THE BOMB AND THE GENERAL

THE BOMB AND THE GENERAL

UMBERTO ECO & EUGENIO CARMI

Translated by William Weaver

Harcourt Brace Jovanovich, Publishers
San Diego   New York   London

Once upon a time there was an atom.

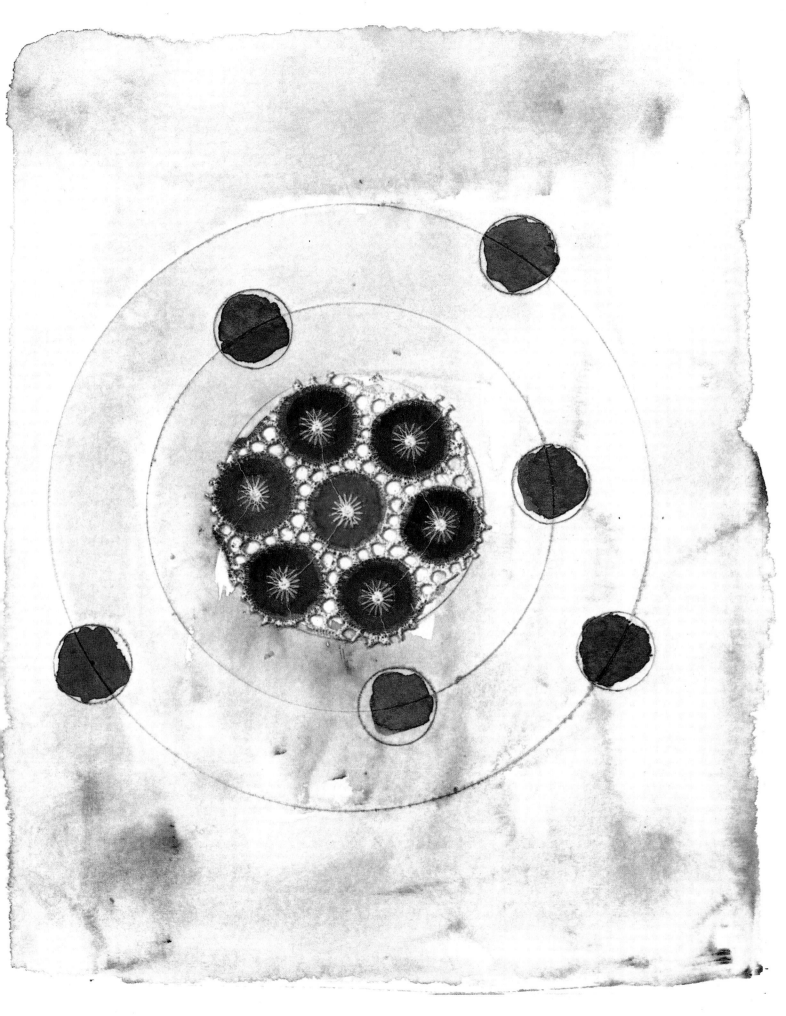

And once upon a time there was
a bad general
who wore a uniform covered with gold braid.

The world is full of atoms.

Everything is made up of atoms.
Atoms are very tiny,
and when they come together
they form molecules
which then
form all the things we know.

Mom is made of atoms.
Milk is made of atoms.
Women are made of atoms.
Air is made of atoms.
Fire is made of atoms.
We are made of atoms.

When the atoms
are in harmony
everything works fine.
Life is based on this harmony.

But when an atom is smashed
its parts strike other atoms
which then strike still more atoms,
and so on . . .

A terrifying explosion takes place!
This is atomic death.

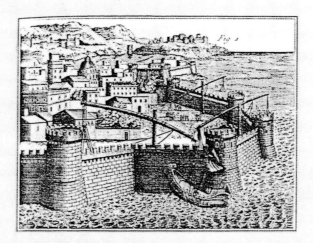

Meanwhile the general
had loaded his bombs on an airplane
and was dropping them one by one
on all the cities.

But when the bombs fell
(empty as they were)
they didn't explode at all!
And the people,
happy at their narrow escape
(they could hardly believe their luck!),
used them for flowerpots.

So they discovered
that life was more beautiful without bombs . . .

. . . and decided not to make any more wars.
The Moms were happy.
So were the Dads.
So was everybody.

And what about the general?
  Now that there were no more wars,
  he was fired.

  And to make use of his uniform with all the braid,
  he became a hotel doorman.
  Since everyone now lived in peace,
  many tourists came to the hotel.
  Even former enemies.
  Even the soldiers whom in the old days
  the general had ordered about.

  When they entered and left the hotel
  the general opened the big glass door
  and made an awkward bow,
  saying, ``Good day, sir.''
  And they
  (who had recognized him)
  said to him with a grim look:
``The service in this hotel is dreadful!
  It's an outrage!''

Hotel

Echelle de ︱————————————————— Toises
1 2 3 4 5 6 7 8 9 10

And the general
turned deep red
and was silent.

Because now he was of no importance at all.

Text and illustrations copyright © 1989 by
Gruppo Editoriale Fabbri, Bompiani, Sonzogno, Etas S.p.A.
English translation copyright © 1989 by
Harcourt Brace Jovanovich, Inc.

Library of Congress Cataloging-in-Publication Data
Eco, Umberto.
[La bomba e il generale. English]
The bomb and the general/by Umberto Eco;
illustrated by Eugenio Carmi.
p.   cm.
Translation of: La bomba e il generale.
Summary: A bad general who wishes to start q war with atom bombs
is foiled and reduced to the humiliating status of doorman,
an occupation in which he can use his uniform with all the braid.
ISBN 0-15-209700-7
[1. War—Fiction.]   I. Carmi, Eugenio, 1920–   ill.   II. Title.
PZ7.E2116Bo   1989
[Fic]—dc19   88-21193

Printed in Italy

First edition

A B C D E

The artwork in this book was done in Windsor and Newton watercolors and collage.
The text type was set in Avant Garde Book Condensed by Thompson Type, San Diego, CA.
The display type is Binner Gothic.
Color separations were made by Gruppo Editoriale Fabbri, Milano, Italy.
Printed and bound by Gruppo Editoriale Fabbri, Milano, Italy
Text design by Camilla Filancia.